11/20

# SERPENTINE

Selected Works by Philip Pullman


THE BOOK OF DUST
*La Belle Sauvage*
*The Secret Commonwealth*

HIS DARK MATERIALS
*The Golden Compass*
*The Subtle Knife*
*The Amber Spyglass*

HIS DARK MATERIALS COMPANION BOOKS
*Lyra's Oxford*
*Once Upon a Time in the North*
*The Collectors*
*The Golden Compass Graphic Novel*

NONFICTION
*Dæmon Voices: On Stories and Storytelling*

# SERPENTINE

## PHILIP PULLMAN

*Illustrations by* TOM DUXBURY

ALFRED A. KNOPF

NEW YORK

THIS IS A BORZOI BOOK PUBLISHED BY ALFRED A. KNOPF

Visit us on the Web! rhcbooks.com

Educators and librarians, for a variety of teaching tools, visit us at RHTeachersLibrarians.com

Library of Congress Cataloging-in-Publication Data is available upon request.
ISBN 978-0-593-37768-0 (trade) — ISBN 978-0-593-37769-7 (ebook)

The text of this book is set in 13-point Baskerville MT Pro.
The illustrations were created using lino-printing and ink.

Printed in Canada
October 2020
10 9 8 7 6 5 4 3 2 1
First American Edition

Ever since Lyra Silvertongue and her dæmon, Pantalaimon, had been reunited, following their terrible parting on the shores of the world of the dead, Lyra had wanted to ask him about the time he'd spent away from her. But she had the obscure sense that she shouldn't ask him directly; he would tell her when he wanted to. However, time went past, and still he didn't, and it began to trouble her.

This feeling came to a head during a

visit she paid to the northern lands, a year after the witch Yelena Pazhets had nearly killed her in Oxford: the time when Lyra had been saved by the birds.

The curse of Bolvangar had been lifted, but the northern lands had still not recovered from the climatic devastation Lord Asriel had caused. However, the retreat of the snows and the loosening of

the permafrost meant that all kinds of archaeological work was possible, and Jordan College sponsored a dig in the region of Trollesund to investigate some recently discovered settlements of the Proto-Fisher people.

Naturally, Lyra demanded to go too; but they made her work. So she slept in a tent and spent days sifting through

the squalid rubbish in a mud-filled midden, while Pantalaimon snapped at mosquitoes; and as soon as the chance came, she begged a ride on the weekly supply-run into the town. She wanted to look at the places she remembered: the sledge depot where she'd bargained with Iorek Byrnison, the dockside where she'd met Lee Scoresby, and the house of the witch consul Dr. Lanselius.

"Two hours, Lyra," said Duncan Armstrong, the graduate student who was driving the tractor, as they drew up outside the General Post Office. "If you're not here at three o'clock precisely, I'll go without you."

"You don't trust us," she said.

"Two hours."

The sledge depot was empty and derelict, but she found Einarsson's Bar, where in the yard next to the alley she'd had her first sight of an armoured bear, and watched Iorek swallowing a gallon of raw spirits and heard him speak of his captivity. The yard looked just the same, with a rusty shack leaning over in a sea of mud. The docks, though, looked very different: the buildings she remembered were half underwater, and new cranes and warehouses had had to be set up further back.

"It's a mess," said Pantalaimon severely.

"Everything's a mess. Let's see if Dr. Lanselius is in."

The consul represented the interests of all the witch-clans, even those who were feuding. Lyra wasn't sure if he'd remember their first meeting, and Pan scoffed.

"Not remember *us*?" he said. "Of course he will!"

"When we first came I'd have been sure no one could forget us," she agreed. "But now . . . I'm not so sure about things."

But he did. Dr. Lanselius was at his door, saying goodbye to a Muscovite amber merchant, and as soon as he saw Lyra and her dæmon he greeted her warmly and showed her into the narrow elegant wooden house.

"Lyra Silvertongue, you're very welcome," he said. "Yes, I know your new name. Serafina Pekkala told me everything about your exploits. Will you take some coffee?"

"Thank you," she said. "She told you everything?"

"Everything she knew."

"Like . . . me and Pan being able to . . ."

Dr. Lanselius smiled.

"Ah," she said, and she and Pan relaxed. It was something they had to be on their guard about all the time. If Dr. Lanselius knew they could separate, there was no need for Pantalaimon to pretend he couldn't leave Lyra's side; and with the consul's permission he leaped out through the open window to explore the garden.

Dr. Lanselius brought the coffee pot and cups into the little parlour, and Lyra asked at once, before Pan came back:

"You know when witches are young, and they do what Pan and I did, they go apart . . ."

"I know a little. Every witch has to go through it, or not live a full witch-life. There are some who can't, or who won't, and their sisters pity them, though those who can't do it pity themselves more. Their lives are not happy."

"What do they do? Where does it happen?"

"In central Siberia there is a region of devastation. Thousands of years ago there was a prosperous city there, the centre of

an empire of craftsmen and traders that reached from Novgorod to Mongolia. But they made war with the spirit world, and their capital was destroyed by a blast of fire. Nothing has lived there since—plant, insect, bird or mammal."

Lyra thought she knew what *the spirit*

*world* meant. It meant another universe, like Will's, or like the world of Cittàgazze. If there had been contact between this universe and another, thousands of years ago, long before the way of cutting through from one universe to another with the subtle knife had been invented, that was very interesting and she wanted to know more; but she reined in her interest quickly, because she didn't want to alert Pan.

She knew exactly where he was and what he was doing, and she didn't want him to stop it. Just at that moment he was investigating the rack of cloud-pine branches outside the consul's house, and trying to divine which of them belonged to Serafina Pekkala's clan, because he had the idea that if he and Lyra tried really hard, they might eventually be able to bypass the alethiometer and discover things by mental power alone. Lyra thought this was crazy, but she was glad he was concentrating on it, because she

didn't want him to overhear her questions to Dr. Lanselius.

"So the witches—the young witches go there with their dæmons, before they're able to separate, and the witches go into this devastated place and the dæmons are afraid to?"

"As I understand it, yes."

Nothing would soften Lyra's memory of the moment she had done a similar thing to Pantalaimon. As she remembered his terrified whimpering puppy-form crouching on the jetty, she felt hot tears of guilt brimming in her eyes, and she could hardly speak. She swallowed several times and said:

"When . . . after the . . . when they've

gone across, and they've found their dæmons again . . . do they talk about it? Do their dæmons tell them what they did when they were apart?"

The witch consul was a shrewd man. His broad and florid face was not expressive, because he had trained himself to be diplomatically non-committal; but he knew when to allow his eyes the animation of sympathy.

"Don't laugh at me," Lyra said, and outside in the mud Pantalaimon pricked up his pine-marten ears.

Dr. Lanselius's own dæmon, a slender serpent, flowed from his shoulder down to the floor, and in a moment or two—the room was not a large one—she had

climbed to the window sill. Both Lyra and the consul were watching her, and when Dr. Lanselius sensed something and relaxed, she felt the change in his attention and looked at him.

"Your dæmon has found plenty to occupy his curiosity," he said. "He won't hear what we say now unless you tell him. But be frank with me; ask me what you want to know."

And Lyra remembered her previous visit to the consul, along with Farder Coram. The old gyptian's guile was equal to the situation, and recalling now what Farder Coram had done, Lyra said:

"I haven't got much time, Dr. Lanselius, and I don't even know the best question to ask. So if you were me, and knowing what you do of what concerns me now, what question would you ask of the Consul of the Witches?"

He smiled, and said, "I remember the last time I was asked that question. How is the excellent Farder Coram?"

"He hasn't been well. He nearly died of pneumonia, but he's recovering. Tell me, Dr. Lanselius! Tell me what question I should ask."

"You should ask the Consul of the Witches to tell you what Serafina Pekkala did in the same case as yours. She had the same doubts."

"Did she?"

"Oh, yes. Her dæmon, Kaisa—and yours,

and every witch's—felt a great betrayal. But witches and their dæmons know that this is to come; they know they'll be tested. You did not. For you and your dæmon it was worse. Nevertheless, Kaisa and Serafina Pekkala suffered too, and she thought his coldness to her afterwards was worse than the suffering of separation itself."

"So what did she do?"

"She waited, and treated him kindly, and said nothing."

"She didn't ask? Even though she wanted to know what he'd done and how he'd managed and everything?"

"Not a word."

"And . . . did he ever tell her?"

"No."

"I thought there were no secrets between us and our dæmons," said Lyra, feeling obscurely hurt.

"Then what are you doing in here, asking me this? Aren't you trying to conceal this from *your* dæmon?"

"No! Not *conceal* . . . I just want to do what's right. Because no one who isn't a witch knows what it feels like . . . And I can't ask anyone but you, because it's a secret, a real deep secret, that Pan and I can do this. I trusted *you*, right, because you know the witches . . . But I've never told anyone else, in this world I mean, not even Farder Coram. And I do want to know what's right, you see. I don't want to put pressure on Pan if I shouldn't. I'd ask

Serafina Pekkala herself if I could, but . . . It's so difficult."

She'd been looking at the coffee pot, and at the floor, and at the tiled stove, and at the bookshelves, but now she looked at his broad and subtle face.

"Yes," he said. "I see that. It's not as if your position was a common one. And I haven't got much comfort for you; all I

can tell you is what those who have experienced the same thing have told me."

"I just have to keep on not knowing," Lyra said unhappily, "and knowing that he's holding something back . . . And the one person I could really talk to about it, who'd really understand every little detail, I'll never see again."

"Not the *only* person."

"Yes," said Lyra firmly.

"Would you like me to pass on a message to Serafina Pekkala for you?"

"Yes . . . No. It's not as if anything important depended on it. It's just my doubt, that's all. Just not knowing. I don't think Serafina would be very impressed by me not being able to put up with that."

"I think she knows what you can put up with. I shall tell her you've come, and give her your greetings, as I assume you'd like me to do."

"Of course. Thank you," said Lyra, hearing a hint of dismissal and gathering herself to stand; but the consul hadn't finished.

"You know, it isn't really surprising that

there are things about ourselves that still remain a mystery to us," he said. "Maybe we should be comforted that the knowledge is there, even if it's withheld for a while."

"There are lots of things we *should* be comforted by," said Lyra, "but somehow it doesn't feel very comforting."

Nevertheless, she felt a little better as she said that, perhaps because she was pleased with herself for putting the thought neatly.

Dr. Lanselius smiled and stood up. "How is your dig progressing?" he asked, opening the parlour door. "Have you made many discoveries?"

"The Proto-Fisher people ate a lot of

fish," she told him, "apparently. But then people still do. The main thing the archaeologists have found out is about the sea level. It was even higher then than it is now."

He tapped the barometer beside the door. "A depression is coming," he said. "And I think it will snow."

"That's good."

"Yes, it is. Things are returning to normal."

Lyra knew without looking that Pan was about to leap on to her shoulder, and she reached up automatically to stroke him. Dr. Lanselius was stooping to pick up his dæmon, the serpent.

"Thank you," Lyra said as she shook hands.

"Be sure to give my greetings to Farder Coram. I have a great respect for him."

"I will. Goodbye!"

The first flurries of snow were swirling in the grey air as they found the tractor outside the General Post Office. Duncan Armstrong was looking at his watch, while his russet ferret-dæmon twitched her nose at Pantalaimon.

"I'm in time," Lyra said. "Just."

"I wouldn't be here if you weren't. Wrap up warm; it'll be a lot colder before we get to the camp."

She clambered into the trailer and settled deep among the furs as Armstrong pressed the starter. The tough little tractor drew away bumpily over the rutted road.

Pantalaimon, coiled around Lyra's neck, spoke closely by her ear to be heard over the roar of the engine.

"You know," he said, "if you hadn't said about us being like witches, he wouldn't have known."

"What? But he did!"

"Only when you told him."

Lyra thought back to what she'd revealed. "Hmm," she said. "But he knew already."

"No he didn't. Serafina never told him that."

"How d'you know?"

"Because his dæmon told me."

Lyra scoffed. "When?" she said. "You were outside all the time!"

"So was she."

"No, she—" Lyra stopped. After she'd seen the little green serpent at the window, her attention had been focused entirely on Dr. Lanselius himself. Then she realised what this meant, and her jaw dropped.

"So *they*—"

"Like us. He's done it too."

"But she said— I mean, what Serafina told you before we found each other again—I thought it was only witches that had ever done it! Witches and us. I thought we were the only ones."

Pan knew full well that *we* included Will.

"Well," he said, "we weren't. And I'll tell you something else."

"Wait. He didn't *tell* me he'd done it, but she *showed* you."

"Yes. So—"

"Maybe we should have done the same. Not told them."

"Yes, just let them see. But the other thing—"

"God, Pan, we've been so stupid! It's a

good thing we can trust him! What other thing?"

"He's Serafina's lover."

"*What?*" She twisted round to look at his face.

He looked defiantly back. "That's right," he said. "They're lovers."

"But he's— I mean— Did she tell you?"

Lyra meant the serpent-dæmon, not Serafina Pekkala, but Pan knew that.

"No," he said. "I just worked it out."

"Oh, well," Lyra said, blowing out her cheeks in scorn, "if you worked it out . . ."

"I'm right."

"You're dreaming."

"I'm right."

"But . . . he's the consul of all the witches, not just Serafina's clan."

"So what?"

"Anyway," Lyra added weakly, baffled, "he's . . . sort of *indoors.*"

"Yeah, and he's very clever and he's very tough."

"But I still don't know how you know!"

"Just something I noticed."

"What?"

"You remember Serafina's crown? Those little scarlet flowers?"

"What about it?"

"Well, he was wearing one in his lapel. And it was fresh. And it's the wrong season."

"There might be all kinds of reasons . . ."

"No, it's a token they have. Witches and their lovers."

They were passing the last houses in the town: wooden buildings mostly one storey in height, with stone chimneys and corrugated iron roofs held down by cables against the winds. The tractor and the trailer swung from side to side through the ruts and potholes.

Lyra wedged herself in more tightly, and pulled the hood of her anorak down further around them both.

"Pan," she said, "if I had something to tell you . . . I mean, if I knew something you didn't . . ."

"I'd know," he said confidently.

"You might not."

"I would. Anyway, you wouldn't be able to keep it to yourself."

"We'll see," she said. "One day I'll find a secret you'll never know about."

"And I bet I'll know it within five minutes."

"All right," she said. "Try this. What was I talking to Dr. Lanselius about?"

"About the dig," he said at once.

"And?"

"The fish bones."

"And?"

"Some other stuff. I don't know. The fact remains that you don't notice anything, and I do."

"Well, I'm glad to hear it."

"Well, I'm glad you're glad to hear it."

"You better be."

The note of the tractor engine changed as they began to climb the slope towards the forest. It wouldn't be nightfall for some hours yet, but the clouds were low and heavy.

"All right back there?" Duncan Armstrong called.

"Fine," she called back.

"It's going to get cold."

"Good!"

Pantalaimon settled more comfortably around her neck.

After a few minutes Lyra said, "You don't know it's a token at all. The flower."

"It doesn't matter," he said, "because he wasn't wearing one anyway. I knew you wouldn't remember."

"All right, enough," Lyra said shakily. "You're being a pain, you know? You're more observant, you're this, you're that, I

never notice anything . . . That's all true, Pan. I know it is. But why *compete*? Why try and make a fool of me? You notice things for me, and I think of things for you. We do what we're good at. We used to be kind to each other. We *are* each other. We shouldn't have secrets. We should tell the truth to each other."

He said nothing, but he wasn't pretending to be asleep. Then he said, "She told me what you were talking about."

"Well then."

"No, not well then. All this time you wanted me to tell you something and you didn't even ask?"

"I was worried in case it wasn't the right time. I didn't want to make you feel you had to. I don't know. This is difficult, Pan. Trying not to ask . . . It never felt easy. But I'd done something horrible to you in the first place and you had the right to keep it to yourself, if you wanted to. But I didn't want you to think I didn't care or I wasn't interested . . ."

"I wouldn't ever think that."

There was another silence, but a more companionable one.

"What *did* she say?" said Lyra. "If she didn't tell you that nonsense about lovers."

"She didn't tell me. I worked it out, and it wasn't the flower. After all—"

"Answer!" she said, and pulled his tail.

"All right. I didn't know what she was talking about at first—I thought she was mad. It was hard to know what to say. She said some people, witches and normal people as well, sort of quarrel with their dæmons. In the end they come to hate each other. They never speak, they try and hurt each other, they just feel contempt, they never touch . . . It's easier for witches because they can put the whole

world between them and their dæmons if they want to. But still they only live half a life, really. And if you're not a witch . . ."

"John the porter at Gabriel!"

"Yeah—like that. Just like that."

One of the porters at Gabriel College never spoke to his dæmon, or she to him. He was a quiet and courteous man, she a bitter-looking terrier. Lyra had been through Gabriel lodge scores of times, and whenever John was on duty there was an air of profound and helpless melancholy under the vaulted stone roof. Coming out of the lodge into the quadrangle was like passing from cold to warm. Lyra hadn't thought of it like that before, but now she shivered, and resolved, next time she went there, to stop and be friendly to the unhappy man and his silent dæmon.

"When I think of what that must be like," she said, "I mean, to get into a state like that, it makes me think of the abyss. That horrible endless bottomless—it must be like having an abyss right next to you every moment, knowing it's there all the time . . . just horrible."

The abyss that opened out of the world of the dead was something that Pantalaimon hadn't seen, but Lyra had told him all about it.

"When I was with Will's dæmon, before she had her name," Pan said, and Lyra rubbed her chin on his head, "we fell in a river and got carried towards a waterfall.

And we saved each other. But the feeling of being swept towards it . . ."

"Pan, d'you think it might have happened at the same time as I nearly fell?"

"It might have done . . ."

"It must have done. Or I'm sure I'd have felt it with you."

"Maybe you falling into the abyss is what made me dizzy. I would have felt it, I know I would."

"Yeah! It must be."

They both fell silent. But this falling was into the loved and familiar, into safety.

"Anyway, she knew what she was talking about, that dæmon," said Lyra. "But I'm glad you're not a snake."

"D'you remember when we saw that mongoose in the museum and I was a snake and Roger's Salcilia was a mongoose, and she couldn't catch me, so I had to let her because they were getting upset?"

Lyra did. The snow was falling thickly now, and it was just the time when the flakes stop looking dark against the sky, because the sky has become darker than they are, so they look light instead. The little tractor's solid rattle sounded muffled in the feathery air. Duncan Armstrong switched on the lights.

"I bet Mary Malone's dæmon would be a snake," Lyra murmured. "She was wise."

"He was a bird. Like a blackbird, or more like a crow with a yellow beak."

"How do you know?"

"I could see him. At the end, just when we got to the Botanic Garden and said goodbye. She can see him now too. Like Will can see Kirjava. I'm sure she can."

Lyra saw no reason to doubt him. She'd been in no state to notice anything at that point; she had been blind with tears and love and sadness. But he was part of her, and he *had* noticed, and she felt proud of him, because not many people had dæmons as clear-sighted as Pantalaimon. She stroked his head and settled down deeper in the furs as they fell asleep.

"Never notice anything," was the last thing she whispered, fondly scornful: "*Ha!*"